RUNAWAY
WOLF PUPS

RUNAWAY WOLF PUPS

EMILY COSTELLO

ILLUSTRATED BY LARRY DAY

AN AVON  CAMELOT BOOK

This is a work of fiction. Names, characters, places, and incidents either are the product of the author's imagination or are used fictitiously. Any resemblance to actual events, locales, organizations, or persons, living or dead, is entirely coincidental and beyond the intent of either the author or the publisher.

AVON BOOKS, INC.
1350 Avenue of the Americas
New York, New York 10019

Copyright © 1999 by Emily Costello
Interior illustrations copyright © 1999 by Avon Books, Inc.
Interior illustrations by Larry Day
Published by arrangement with the author
Library of Congress Catalog Card Number: 99-94826
ISBN: 0-380-79757-7
www.avonbooks.com

First Avon Camelot Printing: November 1999

CAMELOT TRADEMARK REG. U.S. PAT. OFF. AND IN OTHER COUNTRIES, MARCA REGISTRADA, HECHO EN U.S.A.

Printed in the U.S.A.

OPM   10   9   8   7   6   5   4   3   2   1

**For Jillian Richardson
and her cat, Rosie**

RUNAWAY
WOLF PUPS

• 1 •

Stella Sullivan sighed happily. The June sun felt good beating down on her shoulders. Her long red hair was damp, which kept her from getting too hot.

Stella and Josie Russell had spent the morning swimming in the river. Now they were slowly walking along the side of the road toward home. Not talking much. Just enjoying the afternoon. Swimming always made Stella feel sleepy and mellow.

It didn't seem to have the same effect on Rufus, Stella's five-month-old puppy. As Stella and Josie moved along at a lazy pace, the puppy ran ahead, straining against his leash, then dashing back to the girls.

"Want to go over to Marisa's?" Josie asked. "I haven't seen the piglets yet."

"Sure," Stella agreed. Marisa Capra's sow, Clementine, had delivered a litter of piglets a few weeks earlier. Stella had already seen them a bunch of times. She loved pigs.

Stella loved animals of all kinds. Furry ones. Fuzzy ones. Wild ones. Wimpy ones. Animals with hooves and claws and flippers.

But Rufus was her absolutely favorite animal.

Stella had raised the puppy from the time he was about two weeks old. He'd been abandoned at a rest stop, so nobody was exactly sure how old or what breed he was. Stella's Aunt Anya said he looked like a Maltese with his black lips, black nose, black eyes, and shaggy white fur.

He had grown to about the size of a soccer ball. It didn't seem like he was going to get much bigger.

Rufus was the first one to reach the Capras' yard. The parking lot in front was full of expensive cars with out-of-state license plates. California. Arizona. Even one from New Jersey.

The Capras ran a bed-and-breakfast, a cozy sort of inn. They kept a few animals because people who came to Montana on vacation wanted to see animals. Marisa and her mom loved their pigs, horses, and goats. They also spoiled them rotten.

Stella and Josie went around the side of the house. Rufus trotted over to a tiny patch of shade near the porch steps. He stood panting with his tongue hanging out.

"I'd better get him some water," Stella said. She was heading up the steps when Marisa burst out of the barn. She ran toward the house. Then she spotted Stella and Josie, and skidded to a stop.

"You guys!" Marisa said. "I'm so glad you're here. We could use your help."

Marisa was breathing funny and she kept blinking. She looked as if she was fighting back tears.

"What's wrong?" Stella asked.

"Clementine escaped!" Marisa said. "Come on!"

Marisa turned back toward the barn, breaking into a run. Josie and Stella hurried after her. Rufus yipped with excitement as he followed along at their heels.

"How'd she get out?" Josie was jogging to keep up with Marisa, but she seemed calm. Josie lived on a cattle ranch. Chasing down runaway cows was nothing out of the ordinary for her. She probably figured catching a pig would be easy.

"Mom had a new pen built for Clemmy," Marisa explained as she stopped to pull open the oversized barn door. "I guess the fence wasn't strong enough. She tunneled under it."

The girls went into the cool, dim barn. Stella caught a whiff of fresh hay and newly cut lumber. Unlike some barns, the Capras' always smelled good. Mrs. Capra kept it spotless.

"Tunneled out, huh?" Josie sounded amused. "Must be some tunnel." Clementine weighed at least 700 pounds.

"It is." Marisa's tone was glum.

"Don't get so bummed out," Josie told Marisa. "We'll get some food and lure her back into the pen. Shouldn't be too hard."

"Clemmy's not the problem," Marisa said. "It's the piglets. They followed Clemmy out into the field. Whenever we get too close, they scatter. They think running away is some kind of game."

"We'll catch them," Stella said.

"You'd better leave Rufus in the barn," Josie told Stella. "He'll only make matters worse."

Marisa nodded briskly. "Put him in Daisy's stall. And hurry up." Daisy was one of the Capras' goats. She must have been out in the fields because her stall was empty.

Stella wanted to protest. Josie and Marisa were acting like Rufus was a bad dog. And he wasn't—at least, not anymore. Stella had been taking Rufus to obedience school ever since her own school let out. He'd learned how to walk on a leash and come when he was called. Now Stella was teaching him how to sit.

Rufus would behave if Stella let him out into the backyard. Stella was sure of it. But bringing the dog along would upset Marisa. And Marisa was already plenty freaked out.

Stella scooped up the puppy with both hands. She gently dropped him over the low wall that enclosed Daisy's stall.

Rufus trotted over to Daisy's water bowl and began lapping noisily.

"Sorry, boy," Stella said. "I promise to be right back."

Marisa and Josie had already hurried out the far barn door. Stella rushed to join them on the patio.

"Mom's going to try and catch Clemmy," Marisa told Stella.

Mrs. Capra was standing in the grass staring at Clemmy. She had a pig snare in one hand.

Clemmy was in the carrot patch, using her substantial snout to uproot the tender vegetables. She grunted happily as she crunched them up—greens and all.

A man was talking to Mrs. Capra. Stella was pretty sure he was a guest at the bed-and-breakfast. He was wearing a white shirt, light-colored pants, and a baseball cap.

The patio was furnished with a bunch of old wicker chairs and sofas painted lavender. They were covered in flowered cushions Mrs. Capra had designed herself. Big wooden planters filled with blooming primroses sat here and there. The place looked peaceful and cozy.

"I hope Clemmy doesn't run over here," Josie said. "It would be good-bye wicker."

Stella watched as Mrs. Capra tiptoed up to Clementine with the pig snare. The snare looked like a rope noose on a metal bar. You were supposed to slip the noose over the hog's snout and pull it tight. Then you could lead the sow around like a dog on a leash. Of course, convincing a 700-pound sow to go somewhere she didn't want to go wasn't always easy.

Clemmy watched Mrs. Capra approach. At the same time, the pig kept right on digging up carrots.

Mrs. Capra got close enough to pet the pig. Then she lost her nerve. She dropped the snare down at her side and shook her head.

"I can't do this," Mrs. Capra said with a sigh.

Clementine trotted a few steps away—trampling several basil plants in the process.

"You almost had her," Marisa called.

"I don't want to hurt her," Mrs. Capra said.

Josie snorted in disgust. "The snare won't hurt her," she called to Mrs. Capra.

Mrs. Capra summoned her courage. She took a step toward Clemmy.

"Suuueeeweee!" The man in the baseball cap let out an ear-piercing shout. He ran toward Clemmy and lunged at her with his hands outstretched.

Clementine stepped sideways.

The man landed in the dirt.

"Mr. Kesner!" Mrs. Capra rushed to help him up. "Are you okay?"

"I—I thought I could take her by surprise." Mr. Kesner spit out a few crumbs of dirt. "I saw it in a movie once."

Mr. Kesner stood up and tried to dust off his pants. Two big circles of mud stained the knees. "Stupid pig," he muttered.

"Clemmy's not the one who's stupid," Josie whispered.

"Mr. Kesner, please come inside," Mrs. Capra said soothingly. "If you change your clothes, I'll see what I can do about that mud. Girls—keep an eye on Clemmy. I'll be right back out."

Josie waited until the grown-ups were inside. Then she turned to Marisa. "What does Clemmy like to eat?"

"Everything," Marisa said.

"Any favorites?"

"Not really."

"Okay, then put some feed in a bucket and bring it here."

Marisa rushed into the barn. A minute later she was back, carrying a white bucket. Josie took the bucket and casually approached the pig.

"Here, Clemmy." Josie rattled the feed. "Come on, girl."

Clementine raised her head. She took a step toward Josie.

Josie backed up. "Come on, girl. Dinnertime."

Clementine took another step toward Josie.

A piglet came out from under the tomato plants. Another emerged from behind a hedge.

Josie smiled with satisfaction. She edged back, still rattling the feed. "Could someone open the gate to the pen?"

Stella ran to get the gate.

Josie led Clementine and the two piglets all the way through the new pen and into the older, more secure one. She poured the feed into the trough. Clemmy grunted happily as she stuck her nose in. Marisa closed the gate behind them.

"Good work!" Stella told Josie.

"Three down," Josie said.

Marisa made a face. "Four to go."

The girls went back to the garden. Stella spotted a couple of piglets stretched out in the cool soil at the base of a pine tree.

Marisa saw them, too. She started to run over to them. Quick as a wink, the piglets got to their feet and took off.

"Slow down," Stella whispered.

The girls waited until the piglets had found a new bed under the tomato plants. This time they approached calmly. The piglets watched them come. Stella scooped one up. Marisa got the other.

Stella's piglet nosed her ear as she carried him back to the pen. It tickled.

Josie had some success, too. One of the piglets came out of hiding to sniff at the carrots Clementine had dug up. Josie grabbed him before he could take a bite.

Marisa looked into the pigpen. Clementine was stretched out on her side. The piglets had crowded up to nurse.

"One, two, three, four, five," Marisa counted. "We're still missing one. Oh—I think it's Bruiser."

Stella knew Bruiser. He was the littlest piglet in the litter, and the one with the most personality. He had a black spot over one eye, and a funny way of grunting while he was nursing.

"Let's find him fast," Stella said. "He's missing dinner."

Stella, Josie, and Marisa went back out into the garden.

"*Bruis*-ser," Marisa called. "Come out, sweetie."

Stella walked up and down the rows of the vegetable garden, peeking under asparagus ferns and bean poles. No Bruiser. Josie scouted the patio. Bruiser wasn't under any of the furniture. Marisa handled the shrubs, but she didn't have any luck either.

Mrs. Capra came back outside. "Oh—you got Clemmy back in. Way to go! Did you find all of the piglets?"

"We're still missing Bruiser," Stella told her.

Mrs. Capra joined the search. They called and walked in circles for an hour.

As time ticked by, Stella began to feel more worried and desperate. She'd searched every inch of the backyard. She was beginning to think they weren't going to find Bruiser. She tried not to think the worst, but Stella knew piglets were fragile. Bruiser wouldn't survive on his own for long.

"I don't understand." Marisa stopped in the middle of the backyard. Her voice was shaking and tears shone in her eyes. "How could he have just vanished?"

Mrs. Capra came up and gave her a hug. "I don't know. Maybe he got out onto the road."

"Mom, don't say that." Marisa was really crying now.

Mrs. Capra sniffled. Now tears started to roll down *her* cheeks.

Stella shot Josie an urgent look. They had to do something to find Bruiser.

"Come on, don't give up," Stella said. She tried to think. If she were a piglet, where would she get lost? "We could let Rufus out," she suggested.

That spring Stella had gone on a mountain lion hunt with her grandfather and his hunting dogs. It had taken some work, but the dogs had sniffed out the lion. Maybe Rufus could do the same thing.

Josie made a doubtful face. "Rufus isn't exactly a bloodhound."

Stella felt defensive again. "I know that," she protested. "I just thought—"

"Don't fight, girls," Mrs. Capra said. "Letting Rufus out isn't a good idea. We're having a new well dug. I wouldn't want Rufus to fall in."

"A well?" Stella repeated.

Marisa was already running back to a spot near the fence. Stella and Josie ran after her.

Mrs. Capra tried to keep up with them.

Summer was the busy time at the park. The place was overflowing with tourists. Every day, thousands of visitors cruised through the wilderness. Something was always going wrong. Kids got lost. RVs got stuck in the mud. Wild animals wandered into campgrounds. Stella was used to her mom coming home late.

"What kind of emergency?" Stella asked.

"The wolves," Anya said. "Romeo's radio collar is broadcasting mortality code."

Stella's heart skipped a beat. "Mortality code?"

"Yeah—it's a special signal the collar sends out whenever the animal wearing it doesn't move for an hour."

Stella felt a low hum of dread. The wolves were special to her. They were gray wolves, wild ones that had just been released into Goldenrock a few months earlier.

Each wolf wore a collar with a small radio transmitter embedded in the leather. Each collar sent out its own signal. Norma and the other wolf biologists tracked the radio signals from an airplane. They were collecting information about the animals' behavior.

Every scrap of data was valuable. The scientists knew next to nothing about how the wolves lived because the animals had been wiped out in the American West seventy years earlier.

Getting permission to bring wolves back had been a huge battle. Anya and Norma had been fighting that battle since before Stella was born. So had Jack, Stella's father. Jack and Norma had actually met at a pro-wolf meeting at Montana University, when they were both in college there.

Stella had joined the fight when she was seven years old. She and her older sister, Cora, had formed an organization called Kids for Pups. They had held rallies to show the politicians and reporters that kids wanted wolves in their national park.

The wolves belonged there. They had been there long before people came along and killed them to make their livestock safer.

Now the battle was over. Stella, her family, and lots of other families like them had actually succeeded in getting wolves brought back to the park. And that meant Stella felt personally responsible for them.

"Romeo is dead?" Stella squeaked. Her fingers were tingling with dread. She was scared of what Anya was about to tell her.

Of all the wolves, Romeo was her favorite. Cora had given him his nickname: Romeo as in *Romeo and Juliet,* the play by Shakespeare. It's a story about a guy and a girl who are *really* in love. Cora had read it in school.

Anyway, Romeo got his name when Norma and the other biologists set him up on a "blind date." They were worried that he might hurt the female wolf they had picked out for him. But it was love at first sight! Naturally, Cora called Romeo's mate Juliet.

The idea of Romeo dead—it made Stella shudder.

"He's probably fine," Anya said quickly. "Chances are that Romeo just dropped his collar somehow. Norma and Mack are checking it out." Mack worked with Norma at the park.

Stella took a deep breath. *Relax,* she told herself. Anya wouldn't tell her Romeo had dropped his collar if she thought something more serious was going on.

Marisa tapped Stella's leg. "Hey—I think Bruiser's squeals are getting weaker."

Stella gave herself a little shake. Now was not the time to get all worried about Romeo. Bruiser needed her. She quickly told Anya about the trapped piglet.

"Try lowering down some mash," Anya suggested. "Put the food in a pail. Don't fill it too deep. The idea is to get the piglet to crawl into the pail, and you don't want him to drown."

"Got it," Stella said. She smiled, thinking Anya's plan sounded good.

"Hurry," Anya added. "This won't work if

Bruiser is too weak to eat. And that will happen fast if he gets cold. Is it wet in the well?"

"I'm not sure."

"Let's hope not. Oh, that's my other line. Call back if you need me."

Stella turned off the phone. Marisa, Josie, and Mrs. Capra were all staring at her. She told them what Anya had suggested.

Marisa and Mrs. Capra rushed into the barn. They came back a couple of minutes later. Mrs. Capra was carrying a pail. Marisa had some rope.

"I'll tie that," Josie offered. "I know some good knots."

Everyone watched while Josie secured the rope to the bucket's handle. Stella noticed that Mrs. Capra was biting her lip. Marisa's thick dark eyebrows were squished together. The two of them looked like they were about to have twin heart attacks.

"This is going to work," Stella said.

Josie held the pail out to Stella. "Good luck."

Stella swallowed nervously. She hadn't realized it was going to be her job to get Bruiser out of the hole without banging him on the head or drowning him in nasty oatmealish goo.

Oh, well . . . *Someone* had to do it.

Stella put the pail down next to the hole. She laid on the grass with just her head and shoul-

ders sticking out over the opening. Then she carefully lowered the pail into the darkness, hand over hand. She took it slow. She wasn't sure how deep the hole was and she didn't want to hit Bruiser.

The rope went slack.

"It's on the bottom," Stella said. She twisted around so that she could see the others.

"Bruiser isn't squealing anymore." Marisa looked like she was about to start crying again.

"Let's give him a minute to get interested in the mash," Stella suggested. "Then we'll lift him up. Hopefully."

She didn't tell the others that Bruiser might

not have the strength to eat. She had an image of Bruiser lying next to the pail, too cold and weak to get up.

One, one-thousand, Stella counted silently. *Two, one-thousand.* She kept going until she got up to sixty, one-thousand. She had no idea what was going on in the hole. It was too dark to see, and Bruiser wasn't making any noise.

"Here goes." Stella took a deep breath and began pulling up the bucket. She knew right away that it didn't have a piglet inside. The bucket was too light.

"Do you have him?" Mrs. Capra asked.

"I don't—" At that moment, the bucket came into view. No Bruiser.

Stella groaned. So did everyone else.

"Try it again," Marisa said.

Stella nodded. She gently lowered the pail. Again, she began counting. She was up to thirty-three, one-thousand when Josie spoke. "I heard something. Something that might have been piglet hooves scratching on a bucket."

"Bruiser climbing in?" Mrs. Capra sounded hopeful.

Stella immediately started lifting the pail. It felt heavier. Her heart flipped with excitement. "I think we—oh!"

"What?" Josie demanded.

"I think Bruiser just jumped out. Or fell out. The pail suddenly got much lighter."

"Put it down again," Josie told her. "Leave it a little longer. And when you bring it up, bring it up as fast as you can. Don't give Bruiser time to jump out."

"Okay." Stella lowered the pail. She tried to hear some sound from Bruiser. Nothing.

"Okay, lift it up, lift it up," Marisa said. "I can't stand it anymore."

Stella took a deep breath. She started lifting—and immediately knew Bruiser was on board. She pulled up the rope as fast as she could. When the pail came into view, Bruiser was inside. He was lying on his side. A big clump of mash was smeared over one eye.

Stella started to giggle.

Marisa reached out and grabbed the piglet. "You bad, bad boy," she cooed.

Stella sat up with a sigh. A happy ending.

Mrs. Capra patted Stella's shoulder.

Marisa smiled at her.

Then they turned their attention to Bruiser. They fussed over him like crazy. Mrs. Capra even kissed his pink snout.

Josie was all business. "Let's put him in with Clemmy. He hasn't eaten in a while."

Mrs. Capra's smile faded. "You're right. Bruiser

is probably starving! You don't think he'll die, do you? After all he's been through?"

"If he still has an appetite, I'm sure he'll be fine," Josie said.

Mrs. Capra held out her arms. "Come to Mommy, Bruiser sweetie," she said in baby talk. "Let's get you something to eat."

Marisa and Mrs. Capra led the way into the barn. Two minutes later, the four of them watched while Bruiser wormed his way into the mound of nursing piglets. Soon he was sucking eagerly.

Stella laughed when she heard his familiar happy nursing grunt. "He seems fine."

Josie nodded. "He definitely has an appetite."

Mrs. Capra was watching Bruiser carefully. "I think I see a scratch on his back. See it?"

Stella squinted at the piglets. They were piled up in pairs, each one with its mouth firmly locked on a teat. Bruiser was hard to see because one of his brothers or sisters had climbed half on top of him.

"I think I might see a tiny scratch . . ." Stella couldn't keep the doubtful tone out of her voice.

Mrs. Capra nodded, as if she were making a decision. "As soon as he's done nursing, I want to take Bruiser in to see your aunt. We can't have that wound get infected."

"Why don't we just put on a little iodine?" Josie suggested. "You don't want to pay Anya for nothing."

"Money is no object," Mrs. Capra said.

"Better safe than sorry," Marisa agreed.

Josie leaned closer to Stella. "Like mother, like daughter," she whispered.

The two of them exchanged smiles. Stella felt 99.9 percent certain Bruiser was fine. But she could tell Mrs. Capra needed to be reassured by Anya's professional opinion.

As soon as Bruiser finished nursing, Marisa climbed into the pen and got him. Everyone piled into Mrs. Capra's truck. Marisa held Bruiser on her lap. Stella had Rufus on her lap. The morning's swim finally seemed to be affecting the puppy. He'd been napping when Stella went to get him out of Daisy's pen. He was still only half awake.

Mrs. Capra made the quick drive into town.

They pulled up to the clinic.

"What's going on here?" Josie demanded.

A TV van was pulled onto the grass in front of the clinic. A man with an oversized TV camera on his shoulder stood talking to a woman wearing an expensive-looking suit.

"Reporters," Josie whispered.

A green Park Service jeep was parked right out

front. A cruiser from the sheriff's office was double-parked next to it. Down the street were two matching white sedans with official Fish and Wildlife seals on the doors.

Stella's heart started to thump, thump. Something was going on. Something not good.

"May I get out?" Stella asked.

"Sure," Mrs. Capra said. "We'll meet you inside as soon as we find a place to park."

Stella hopped out of the truck. She carried Rufus up the walkway, snaked past the reporters, and went into the waiting room.

The small room was crowded with people. They didn't look like Anya's clients. One clue: they had no pets with them. The adults looked up as Stella came in.

Stella saw Assistant Sheriff Rose. She was the one who'd found Rufus early that spring. Sheriff Rose gave Stella a little wave. Stella waved back, moving quickly through the room. She peeked into Anya's office. It was empty. Stella put Rufus down and closed him inside.

Now she could hear muffled voices coming from one of the exam rooms. She went down the hall and cautiously looked inside.

Anya, Norma, and Mack were huddled around the table. They were dressed for surgery in blue gowns. They were talking in low voices.

But something was wrong. The adults were oddly still. Their hands weren't moving. They weren't operating.

The adults were so engrossed they didn't notice when Stella took another step into the room. Now she could see what was on the table. A wolf. And Stella recognized him. It was Romeo.

This was bad. Very bad. Norma never would have brought Romeo here unless he was in rough shape.

But Stella's first impression wasn't of a sick animal. It was of a majestic, powerful one. Even lying still in this alien place, Romeo was beautiful. He had dark gray fur. The dense, luxurious stuff glistened under the bright light. His head and paws seemed almost too big, like he hadn't grown into them yet.

There was only one problem. Romeo *was* lying still—unnaturally still. Even a creature that's

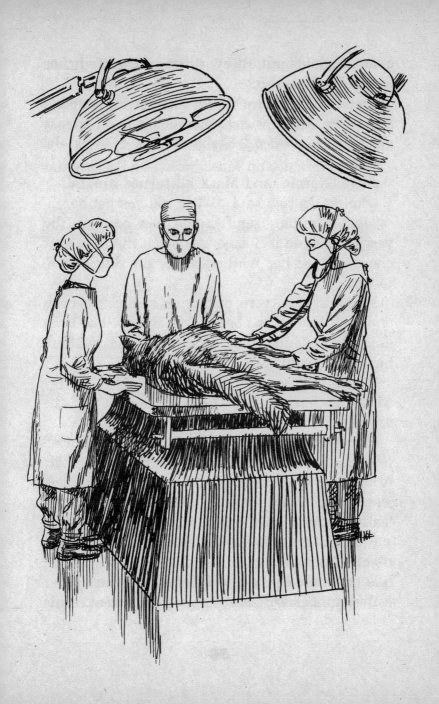

been drugged for surgery moves a little. Twitches a muscle. Something.

Stella felt as if ice water was flowing through her veins. What was Romeo doing here? *Please don't let him be dead,* Stella thought desperately.

"Mom?"

Anya, Norma, and Mack all turned around.

"Stella," Norma said. "When did you get here?"

"Just a minute ago." Stella had been on the verge of asking if Romeo was dead. But now that she could see her mother's face, she didn't have to ask.

Norma's eyes were puffy and red. She'd been crying. If Romeo had been alive, if there had been any small chance of saving him, Norma wouldn't have let herself take the time to cry.

Stella felt as if someone had put a heavy weight on her chest. Romeo . . . dead. It was too awful to believe.

Someone came up behind Stella. She glanced over her shoulder. It was Assistant Sheriff Rose. A man was standing behind her. He had on black jeans and a T-shirt. He also was wearing a leather holster with a gun in it.

Stella took a step away. The man's manner was highly intimidating. He had this intense gaze, like he would know if you dared to lie to him.

Assistant Sheriff Rose cleared her throat. "This

here is Special Agent Pete Morehouse. He's with Fish and Wildlife."

"Can we come in?" Morehouse's voice was no-nonsense, like an Assistant Principal's. "Got a few questions to ask."

"Sure," Mack said.

Morehouse and Assistant Sheriff Rose crowded into the cramped room. They took out small notebooks and pens. Morehouse asked most of the questions. Stella listened in horror as the details slowly came out.

Mack and Norma had followed Romeo's mortality code to a remote pass on Mount Edna. He was still alive, shot twice, and he'd lost a lot of blood. Bringing him to the clinic was a last-ditch effort. They'd had to take him out by helicopter. By the time they got to the clinic, it was already over. He died somewhere along the way.

Special Agent Morehouse flipped his notebook closed. "We'll take it from here." He pointed to the wolf. "I'm afraid he's evidence. I'll get one of my guys to come and get him."

Assistant Sheriff Rose held a hand out to Norma. "We're going to find out who did this," she said solemnly.

"Thanks," Norma said in a flat tone.

Stella had to fight an urge to roll her eyes. She knew Assistant Sheriff Rose meant well. But finding the shooter wasn't really the point. Punishing some stupid wolf-hater wouldn't bring Romeo back.

Anya sighed and rubbed her eyes. "What happened with the pig?"

Pig? Oh, right—Bruiser. Stella forced a smile. "We got him out of the well. But Mrs. Capra's worried about a scratch on his back. She brought him in."

"Okay. I'd better go look."

"I think I'm going to go, too," Mack said. "Maybe take a walk." He seemed edgy. Anxious to get away.

"Okay, Mack. We'll be seeing you." Norma didn't meet Mack's gaze. She was still looking down at Romeo. Her expression was faraway.

"Stella." Mack gave her a nod as he slipped out the door.

After he was gone, Stella went over and wrapped her arms around her mother's waist. "Mom? You okay?"

There was a long pause before Norma answered. "So many years . . . We fought for so many years just to get the right to bring wolves back to Goldenrock. Now it looks as if all that work was for nothing. The wolf-haters are going to win in the end. They'll just pop off the wolves one at a time."

Stella felt tears flood her own eyes. Her mom sounded choked up. Hearing her mother cry made her feel awful. Kind of vulnerable and scared. Norma was usually so strong.

"Did they shoot Juliet, too?"

"No," Norma said. "But the signals from her collar suggest she may be denning."

Stella drew back in surprise. "You mean she's going to have pups?"

She almost couldn't believe it when her mother nodded. It was strange under the circumstances, but Stella felt a surge of excitement.

All of the scientists involved with the reintroduction had been very interested in when the wolves would produce pups. They had all agreed it wouldn't happen this year. The scientists were certain the trauma of being moved from Canada to Montana would curb any urges the wolves might feel to reproduce.

The possibility that Juliet was denning was great news. But Norma wasn't smiling.

"Aren't you glad?"

Norma gave her a sad smile. "Worried mostly. And I need you to keep this a secret."

"How come?"

"Because Juliet and her pups, if there are any, are in a dangerous situation."

"You think someone might try to shoot the

pups?" Stella couldn't imagine anyone being that cruel.

"Yes—or Juliet. And there's another problem. Remember, father wolves usually help raise the young. One parent stays with the pups. One goes out to hunt. Now that Romeo is dead, Juliet won't have any choice but to leave her pups—"

"If there are any."

"Right. If Juliet has pups, she'll have to leave them alone while she hunts. That means predators will have a chance to gobble them up."

"Including human predators?"

"Right."

Now Stella felt worried, too. She jumped when Anya appeared in the doorway. She looked stressed-out.

"Is something wrong with Bruiser?" Stella demanded.

"No. He's fine. It's Marisa and Mrs. Capra. One of the reporters told them about Romeo. They're both bawling out in the waiting room. Josie couldn't take it. She headed home on foot."

Norma let out a low chuckle. "You're not going to get rid of them for days."

"Weeks," Stella said. She smiled along with her aunt and mom. But the truth was, she felt like crying, too. And she knew Norma and Anya felt the same way.

Stella was getting dressed the next morning when the doorbell rang. "Cora—can you get that?" she called.

No answer. Then Stella remembered. Cora was off at a rodeo with her best friend and her family. "Great," Stella muttered.

She pulled a T-shirt over her head, banged down the stairs in her bare feet, and threw open the door. Jared, a boy who had been in Stella's class the year before, was standing on the stoop.

The minute the door was open, Jared popped into the front hall. His hair looked a little wild. So did his expression. "We need your help!"

"We?"

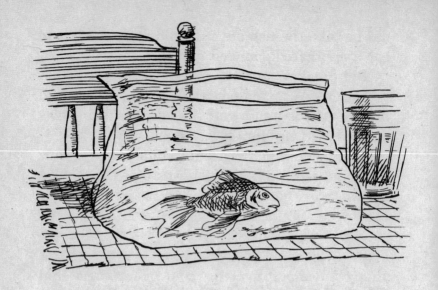

Jared held up a Ziploc storage bag. The gallon size. Big enough to hold a big pot of leftover stew.

Inside the bag was a goldfish. Its reflection through the plastic was like an intense orange glob. Stella saw one glistening black eye, and she had the distinct impression the goldfish was looking at her.

"Smokey attacked her!" Jared was acting as if he had just finished a two-liter bottle of soda all by himself. Jumpy. Frazzled.

"Who's Smokey?"

"My neighbor's cat. He scooped the fish right out of the pond with his paw. I saw him do it. Then he just put the fish down on the grass. Why did he take the fish out if he didn't even want to eat him?" Jared sounded outraged.

"Did Smokey hurt the fish?"

"Did he? What do you think? That he yanked him out of the pond with his needle-sharp claws *without* hurting him?"

Stella peered more carefully into the bag. Now she could see where the fish was injured. Ragged pieces of fish flesh floated out from a gash in the fish's side. Stella didn't see any blood. But the gash was plenty deep.

"I called the pet store for help," Jared said. He still sounded aggravated. "The woman there said maybe it was time for the goldfish to go to the big fishbowl in the sky. Maybe his time is up, she said. Is that supposed to be funny? Because I am not laughing here!"

They were still standing in the front hall. Stella closed the door and led Jared into the kitchen. "Let's call Anya," she suggested.

"That's why I'm here. I tried calling the clinic, but she didn't answer." Jared sank into a kitchen chair. He put the bag down on the kitchen table. The bag changed shape, but it didn't open.

"I'm not surprised. She's supposed to be out at Quick Silver Ranch debudding calves."

Debudding is ranch lingo for removing a calves' horns—a job that's done soon after they're born.

Stella knew it was the kind of work that completely absorbs your concentration. For one thing, it involves separating the calves from their mothers. Most cows didn't mind, but once in a while, one would get mad. And an angry 600-pound cow wasn't the kind of creature you wanted to turn your back on.

Stella picked up the phone and punched in Anya's cell phone number. Three rings. And then a click. "Hello. The cellular customer you've reached can't come to the phone."

Stella waited for the recording to end. Then she left Anya an urgent message, explaining about the fish.

"I'm sure she'll call back soon," Stella said.

Jared was examining the fish. "I don't think we can wait that long. The goldfish is having a hard time breathing."

"How do you know?" Stella looked, too. She immediately realized Jared was right. The goldfish's gills seemed to be staying open an extra long time. His mouth was open, too, as if he was gasping for air. Can fish gasp?

"Come on, come on," Jared said, hopping to his feet. "We have to do something fast."

"Like what?" Stella demanded.

Stella's father wandered into the kitchen. Jack was carrying an empty coffee cup and had that faraway look he sometimes got after spending hours writing. He went straight for the coffeemaker and yanked out the pot.

"Hey kids. What are you doing?"

"Trying to save this fish. Do you know anything about fish?"

"Jared, my dad is a writer," Stella said. "He's the only person in my family who doesn't know anything about animals."

Jack looked slightly hurt. "Well, I know a little about research."

"That's true . . ." Stella wasn't sure where her father was going with this. But she felt bad for maybe hurting his feelings.

"Why don't you kids use my computer to get some help on the World Wide Web? I could use a break anyway."

Jared was already to the door. "Let's go."

"Bring the fish," Stella said. "That way we can keep an eye on him while we work."

They hurried back into the office. Jared put the goldfish down next to the monitor. He was still doing his fishy gasps. No better. No worse.

Stella booted up the Web browser. She typed in "goldfish" and "injuries." They waited a few seconds while the search engine worked.

"Two thousand sixty-five pages!" Jared moaned.

"It'll take us the rest of the week to read all of those."

"Then we better get started." Stella clicked a button to load the first Web page. The computer began to work. "Connecting to HTTP server . . ."

When the page finally came up, it turned out to be the home page of some woman who had put up pictures of her pets—three perfectly healthy-looking goldfish. The woman was the one who had been injured. She had a broken arm.

"This is useless," Jared complained.

Stella clicked back to the search engine and then pressed a button to load the second Web page. Images immediately began to pop up on the screen.

"Bingo," Jared said with satisfaction. The Web page seemed like just what they needed. It described what to do in the case of all kinds of goldfish injuries—including fishy flesh wounds.

"I'll print this out," Stella said.

She clicked a button. The printer moaned to life. Pages started rolling out. Stella grabbed them.

Jared picked up the bag. "Where are we going to operate?"

"Kitchen table," Stella suggested. "Is that okay, Dad?"

"Sure."

Stella read from the list. "We need a slotted spoon, a big bowl, some medicine from the bathroom, an alarm clock—"

"I'll get the stuff in the kitchen," Jack offered.

"Take the list." Stella held it out to him. "I'll get my alarm clock," she added.

"Don't we need a towel?" Jared said. "Where can I find one?"

"Look in the laundry room," Stella told him.

Everyone ran in a different direction. A few minutes later, they were back in the kitchen. Stella checked items off the printed list. "I think we have everything," she said.

"Set the clock for sixty seconds," Jared said. "You have to complete the operation in that amount of time, or the fish will die from lack of oxygen."

"I know," Stella said tensely.

"I'll start the clock," Jack told her. "Are you ready?"

"As ready as I'll ever be," Stella said.

"On your mark, get set, go!" Jack reached over and started the clock.

• 5 •

Jared opened the bag. He scooped the goldfish out with a slotted spoon, and placed it on top of a towel Stella had moistened and laid on the kitchen table.

Stella tried to be calm. Anya was always calm when she was operating. Always. It was so quiet in the kitchen Stella could hear the clock ticking. Tick, tick, tick.

Concentrate, Stella told herself. This was a life-and-death situation. Of course, the life in danger was a goldfish's. But still, the goldfish deserved help. He, she, it, whatever—who could tell?—seemed so pitiful. Especially now that it was out of the water. The fish's gills were working uselessly. And it was staring at Stella with one dark eye.

Besides, Jared seemed wrapped up in this fish. Stella didn't want to let him down.

She picked up a Q-tip and gobbed antibiotic ointment all over it. Then she gently applied the ointment to the deep gash on the fish's side. The information from the Web said that would keep the wound from getting infected.

"Okay, I'm done," Stella said.

"What about the other side?" Jared asked.

"What about it?"

"I think the fish has a wound on his other side, too."

Stella glanced at the clock. She still had about twenty seconds. "How am I going to flip him?"

"Should I get a spatula?" Jack asked.

"No," Jared said quickly. "He's not a fillet of fish. Let me do it." He picked up a corner of the towel and sort of jerked it. The goldfish flopped over on its other side.

Sure enough, there was a deep gouge just behind the goldfish's front fin. Stella squeezed more ointment onto the Q-tip and covered up the wound.

"Five seconds," Jack warned.

Stella picked up the towel. She tossed the fish back into the bowl of water they had waiting. It hit the water with a splash and began to sink.

"Oh, no," Jared said.

"This doesn't look good," Jack said.

Stella watched silently as the fish sank all the way to the bottom. It rested there.

"Is he dead?" Jack asked.

"I don't think so," Jared said. "His gills are working."

It was true. If Stella really concentrated she could see the fish's gills moving in and out ever so slightly—almost as if they were caught in a breeze.

"I think he's in shock," Stella said.

"From the cat attack?" Jared said.

"Maybe," Stella said. "Or maybe we kept him out of the water too long."

"Why don't you resuscitate him?" Jack asked.

"How?" Stella asked.

"Follow the directions." Jack waved the pages they had printed around in the air. "It's all right here in black and white."

"Okay. What do I do?"

"Scoop the fish up in its net," Jack read.

"Dad, we don't have a net."

"Improvise! The little guy is dying here."

"Use the spoon," Jared suggested.

"Okay," Stella said nervously.

"Scoop him up in the net—or the spoon," Jack read.

Stella handed Jared the spoon. "You do it. I don't think that fish likes me."

Jared took the spoon and managed to get it under the fish.

"Bring the fish to the top of the tank—um, mixing bowl," Jack read.

Jared carefully lifted the fish up.

"Wave the net slowly back and forth on the top of the tank so that water rushes over the fish's gills," Jack read.

Jared slowly began moving the spoon back and forth. He looked like a magician waving a wand over a top hat.

Stella peeked over his shoulder. The fish didn't look any different. "Now what?" she asked her dad.

"We're supposed to do that for five minutes or until the fish recuperates," Jack said.

"What if he's not better in five minutes?" Stella asked. The fish didn't look that good to her. He seemed to have lost some of his color—or could that have been her imagination?

"Let's not lose hope," Jack said.

"Listen," Jared said. "If he's going to die, I want to know I did everything possible to help him."

Jack gave Jared a pat on the shoulder. "Then just keep waving him back and forth. We'll let you know when five minutes are up."

Five minutes doesn't *sound* like a long time. When you're doing something enjoyable, like watching a movie, five minutes flies by. But Stella wasn't exactly *enjoying* watching Jared wave his arm back and forth.

She felt like they had been in the kitchen for days. Especially since she couldn't see any sign that the waving was doing anything to help the fish. He looked exactly the same. Too still. And a bit faded.

"And . . . time," Jack said.

"Whew!" Jared said. "Not a second too soon. My arm is about to fall off."

Stella held her breath as Jared slowly lowered the fish into the mixing bowl and removed the spoon. The goldfish sank. He lay on the bottom for a second. Then Stella saw one of his side fins wave. He moved forward a tiny bit. Then his other side fin started working. He moved a little more.

"He's swimming!" Jared said.

By the time the words were out of his mouth, it was true. The goldfish's powerful back fin had gotten into the act. He was moving quickly now.

Stella gave Jared a big smile. "You did it!"

"I know," Jared said. He looked happy for about one second. Then a shadow passed over his face. "Listen, can I leave the goldfish here overnight? I think he needs a little rest. And I have to get home right now."

"Why? Did you forget to feed Harley or something?" Harley was Jared's iguana. He used to be the classroom iguana, but then he got sick, and Anya talked Jared into giving him a quieter place to live.

"No, of course I didn't forget to feed Harley." Jared seemed insulted by the suggestion—even though he had to know that Stella was joking.

"So what's the big rush?"

"I have to talk to my neighbor about putting a screen over his pond. I don't want to go through *this* again."

Stella smiled. "Dad? Is it okay if the goldfish sleeps over?"

"Sure," Jack said. He'd retrieved his coffee mug and filled it. Now he was fussing with the milk and sugar.

"Thanks. See you!" Jared let himself out the kitchen door.

"Leave the milk out," Stella said. "I'm going to have cereal."

Jack nodded absently. "You know, I like that kid. His heart is in the right place."

Stella shrugged. She was hungry.

Stella was working on her second bowl of Cheerios when the back door opened. Norma and Mack stomped in, and paused to take off their big boots. Stella hadn't seen her mother since after dinner the night before. Norma had announced that she was going into the office to check on Juliet's radio signal. Apparently, she had been in the office all night long.

"What did you find out?" Stella asked.

Jack got up from the table. "You guys look like you could use some coffee."

"Thanks." Norma sat heavily at the table. She glanced at the goldfish in the mixing bowl. But she didn't seem too curious about what it was doing there. "Long night."

"None for me," Mack said with a wave of his hand. "I'm on my way home to go to bed."

"What did you find out?" Stella repeated.

"Juliet's barely moving," Norma reported.

"We tracked her all night," Mack said. "She didn't move more than ten feet."

"So she's denning," Stella said.

"Probably," Mack said.

"Are you sure you don't want a cup of coffee?" Jack asked Mack. "Or something to eat? You've got a long drive."

"You could take a nap on the couch," Norma suggested.

"Well—maybe a cup of coffee isn't such a bad idea," Mack admitted.

Stella squirmed. How could the adults talk about *coffee* at a time like this? Didn't they realize she needed to know what was happening with Juliet?

"What do you mean *probably?*" Stella asked impatiently.

Mack sighed. "Could be a false pregnancy."

"A what?"

"Thanks," Norma said as Jack put a mug of coffee down in front of her. She leaned forward and inhaled. "That smells like heaven."

"Mom, what is a false pregnancy?" Stella was losing patience.

Norma took a sip. "Juliet may think she's pregnant even if she's not. If that's true, she'll build a den just like any pregnant wolf would."

"Sounds weird," Stella said.

"It's not unusual in wolves," Mack said. "And I think it's more likely to be a false pregnancy than a real one, considering that it's June—late for wolves to be giving birth."

"How can we find out for sure?" Stella asked.

"Well, seeing some pups would clear up the mystery," Norma said.

"You going to hike out to Mount Edna?" Jack asked.

"Not me," Mack said quickly. "I'm going to bed. I only got about three hours' sleep last night. On a cot."

"We could go tomorrow," Norma said reluctantly. " 'Course, if she does have pups, she's been nursing. And if she's nursing, it would be nice if we could drop some roadkill for her to eat. Making milk makes you awfully hungry."

"We should find out for sure," Mack admitted.

"I could go with you." Stella sat up straighter. "Please Mom? We have to know if Juliet has pups! *I* have to know. Aren't you curious?"

Norma gave Stella a wink. "Totally."

"So we can go? Today? Please? I'll pack us a lunch. What kind of sandwich do you want?"

Norma looked at Jack. Some silent signal seemed to pass between them. "Tuna," she said. "And put in some cheese and cookies. It's a rough hike."

"All right!" Stella said.

An hour later, Norma and Stella were in Norma's truck. Norma drove down the road that went to Josie's house. A few miles later she took a turn onto a little-used road that led into Goldenrock. After half a mile, she pulled off to the side.

"Here?" Stella asked. Somehow it was surprising that Juliet was this close to home. She'd imagined the wolf den deep inside the park. Somewhere safer.

"Mount Edna," Norma said matter-of-factly. "About half of the mountain is in the park. The south side is all private land."

Stella got out of the car. She spun in a circle. "Who does that land belong to?"

"Got to be the Russells'."

Stella felt a tinge of anxiety. Somehow this felt like bad news. The Russells—that was Josie's family. Josie was Stella's best friend. But Josie's father was completely opposed to the wolf reintroduction. And her brother, Clem, was even worse. He'd even tried to ruin a pro-wolf rally that Cora and Stella had held earlier that spring.

"The park side of Mount Edna is rugged," Norma said. "I want you to stay right behind me."

Stella nodded. She had her own backpack with a knife, compass, flashlight, whistle, and half of the food and water. She wasn't planning to get separated from her mother, but she was prepared, just in case.

Norma plunged into the forest.

Stella hurried after her. She held out one hand to stop the twigs that snapped back into her face. "Mom? Who do you think shot Romeo?"

"No idea."

"Could have been Clem." Clem lived nearby, and he was the sort of person who would be proud to kill a wolf. He's someone who would brag about it.

"Stella." Norma turned around and faced her. "I don't want to hear you say that again. You have absolutely no proof that Clem was involved."

"He lives on the other side of this mountain!"

"That's not proof. And you can't go around accusing people of crimes. Understand?"

"Sure," Stella said meekly. But it was hard to get the thought out of her mind. Clem—it just seemed so obvious. She wondered if Assistant

Sheriff Rose would question him. Or Agent Morehouse.

The land began to slope upward, gently at first and then more steeply. There was no real trail. Stella felt as if she were climbing a set of stairs that never ended. Up, and up, and up, and up.

Ten minutes later, Stella was covered in sweat and breathing hard. Each breath she took was a lung buster. Her legs were aching. They kept climbing. Up and up.

The trees and ferns pressed in on her and tripped her. Twigs snapped in her face. She had to negotiate around trees. Flies were attracted to her sweat and buzzed in her ears.

"How are you doing, Muffin?"

"Fine!"

At last Norma found a small creek bed for them to hike along. Here there was less vegetation. But the rocks were wet and slippery. Stella used her hands to pull herself up. Pretty soon the knuckles on one hand were scraped and bloody. They kept climbing. Up and up.

Mount Edna wasn't a tall mountain. If there had been a trail, climbing it would have been simple. But there wasn't a trail.

For the first time, Stella realized that someone—forest rangers, Native Americans, or trappers—made all of the trails she usually hiked on.

And she was grateful for those people, whoever they were. Because hiking without a trail was *work*.

Another twenty minutes passed. Up and up.

Norma sat down on a huge boulder and pulled out a map. Stella leaned against the rock; resting. She waited while Norma studied the map. The spots where the biologists had pinpointed Juliet's radio signal were plotted on it.

"We're close," Norma said. "Let's eat some lunch and then see if we can find Juliet's den."

"Great." Stella was starving—and thirsty. Especially thirsty. She pulled out the water and drank down half the bottle. Then she got out the food and went to work. Tuna on rye bread had never tasted better.

Norma put away the map and helped herself to some water. "We're up high enough," she said. "Now we just have to see if we can find the den."

"Is it going to be hard to find?"

Norma chuckled. "Probably. But let's worry about that after lunch."

Stella and Norma each ate a big sandwich, a hunk of cheese, a handful of baby carrots, and two cookies. Normally Stella would have been ready for a nap after such a feast, but the thought of finding Juliet and the pups made her feel wide awake.

Norma seemed to feel the same way. She cleaned up quickly and put on her pack. "Let's head out."

"Great."

"See if you can find some wolf tracks," Norma said.

They moved at a different pace now, ambling through the trees, heads down. Norma paid special attention to any part of the woods where the ground was packed down.

Stella knew that animals create trails through the woods just like humans do. They're called game trails. A herd of elk might take the same path through a forest each evening during the summer. Predators used game trails, too. And so did hunters.

Hikers usually didn't. Game trails never headed straight up a mountain, and hikers were usually focused on getting to the summit.

Thanks to the map, Norma had a good idea of where Juliet had been hanging out. Within about ten minutes, she'd spotted some wolf prints in the moist soil near the creek.

"These look fresh."

Stella crouched down for a closer look. "They look like dog prints to me."

"That's true," Norma said. "But I doubt any big dogs have been up here for months." She got up and followed the prints. "And look at this. These prints continue in a straight line. Purposeful. Like a hunter. Dog tracks usually dart all over the place."

"Are we going to follow them?"

"Follow them *back*," Norma said. "These tracks are leading away from the area Juliet has been sticking close to. We want to see where she was coming from. Not where she was going."

Norma walked along slowly. She made a soft breathy grunting noise that made Stella giggle.

"What are you doing?"

"Imitating the sound mother wolves make when returning to their dens."

"I don't think you're going to fool them."

But ten minutes later, Stella heard a sound. A breathy grunting sound not unlike what her mom was making. Her first thought was that it was Juliet. Then she realized—it was the pups.

There *were* pups.

Wild wolf pups.

Born right here on Mount Edna.

Stella couldn't stop smiling. This never would have happened if Norma and Jack and Anya hadn't believed it could happen, and fought for it.

Norma bent down low next to a hollowed-out tree. "Look at this," she whispered.

Stella knelt down next to her mother. She

peeked into the tree trunk. It was dark. At first, Stella thought the ground was boiling. The wolf pups were a mass of wiggling fur.

"Oh. Oh—wow."

"They're probably about four days old," Norma whispered.

"There are so many."

"Let's try to count them," Norma said. "This is a historic event. I'm going to have to make a full report."

Stella tried counting faces. Then tails. But the wolf pups were full of energy. They were climbing all over each other.

"I think there are seven," Norma said.

Stella shook her head. "Eight. I think."

"It's hard to tell . . . Hey, come on. We'd better get back to town. I've got to call Mack. And maybe we can get some roadkill up here somehow."

Stella was ready. She didn't want Juliet to come back and find a couple of humans staring at her pups. Besides, who cared exactly how many there were? The important thing was that they *existed*.

Norma led the way down the mountain.

Stella crashed after her.

"I can't believe Romeo and Juliet managed to

mate!" Norma burst out. She sounded as excited and full of wonder as Stella felt.

"It's incredible. Just great!" Stella loved sharing such a happy moment with her mother. Especially after what had happened yesterday with Romeo. Had it really been yesterday? So much had happened since then.

"And it must have happened while they were still in the pen." Norma turned back and gave Stella a smile. "I guess being penned up wasn't as stressful as we thought!"

"I guess not."

"Of course, these pups *are* late. Seven of them!"

"Eight."

"Juliet won't be able to raise such a big litter on her own. Not now that Romeo is dead." Norma sounded more somber now.

Stella imagined how awful they'd feel if the pups died—slowly starved in the woods. And all because some stupid human had killed their father. "Won't the roadkill help?"

"I don't think it's enough," Norma said slowly. "Maybe we should bring Juliet and the pups back to a pen in the park."

"Bring her back?"

"That way we can help Juliet feed the pups. Then, when they're old enough, we can release them all. One happy family." Norma sounded rather pleased with her plan.

"How are you going to get Juliet and the pups back to the pen?"

"It'll be easy. Just leave it to me."

• 7 •

Stella was hungry again by the time Norma pulled the truck into the driveway. Climbing that mountain had been hard work.

Jack was already working on dinner. Cora wouldn't be back for a couple of days. May's family had taken her to Frontier Days, a big rodeo in Cheyenne, Wyoming.

Stella set the table while Norma made a few phone calls and told Jack about the pups.

Norma came back into the kitchen in time to help pour drinks. "Mack's going to call the troops," she reported. "There'll be a big debate before we decide whether to bring Juliet and the pups in. I turned the ringer off so that we could eat in peace."

They took forty-five minutes to gobble down Jack's special pasta with sausage-and-pepper sauce. After the meal, Norma picked up her messages.

"I've got to go into the office," Norma announced. "Everyone involved with the reintroduction is going to meet and talk about what to do with Juliet."

"You've got to talk them into helping her," Stella said.

"We'll see," Norma said.

Stella gave her mom a kiss good-bye. She helped Jack clean up the dinner dishes and took Rufus for a walk. Images kept popping up in her mind. Romeo at the clinic. The wolf pups squirming around in their den.

She was worried about Juliet and the pups. Worried about all the reintroduced wolves. Surviving in the wild was hard enough, with the dangers of starvation, cold, and injuries. Wild animals had enough problems without hunters making things worse.

What if all the work they'd done to bring back the wolves was useless? Or worse than useless. What if they'd only gotten the wolves returned so that the wolf-hunters could gun them down?

With so much on her mind, Stella didn't think

she'd be able to sleep until Norma came home. But she drifted off the second she closed her eyes.

The next morning, Stella got up and hurried down to the kitchen.

Jack was reading the paper.

"Where's Mom?"

"Not home yet," Jack said.

"They're still meeting?" Stella asked.

Jack laughed. "No. She called late last night. There was a long debate, but everyone eventually agreed it was best to bring Juliet and the pups in. Norma and Mack went out to Mount Edna to lay a trap for her."

Stella smiled. "Great."

"She said she'd call as soon as there was some news."

Stella settled in to wait for a call, for word that Juliet was okay, that the pups were okay. She wanted to know that the bad guys hadn't won this round.

She'd just popped two pieces of bread into the toaster when the phone rang. "I'll get it!" she yelled, hoping it was Norma. "Hello?"

"Stella?"

"Yeah—hi, Aunt Anya."

Anya laughed. "Why do you sound so disappointed?"

"I was hoping you were Mom." Stella explained about Juliet and the pups.

"I doubt she's going to call anytime soon," Anya said.

"Why not?"

"Well, think about it. She and Mack have to modify a trap so it won't hurt Juliet. Then they've got to gather up a bunch of radio equipment, hike up the mountain, and settle in to wait. Juliet's not going to appear just because they want to catch her. Remember how it was when we tracked that mountain lion?"

"Yes." In fact, it had taken three tries before they'd had any success.

"Listen, why don't you spend the day with me?" Anya asked. "I'll keep you busy. And that should keep your mind off the wolves."

"Okay," Stella agreed immediately. Spending time with Anya was practically her favorite thing in the world. "Where are we going?"

"The Homesick Ranch," Anya said. "Pick you up in fifteen."

Stella pulled on an old pair of jeans and boots and told Jack where she was going. She was waiting in front of the house when Anya's big green truck pulled up.

"Is there a sick animal at the Homesick Ranch?" Stella asked once they were on the road.

"Nope," Anya said. "Just routine stuff. Branding. Vaccinations. Ear tags."

"Wow," Stella said.

The annual roundup and branding was an important event on ranches. Stella had always been fascinated by the process. She'd begged Josie to let her watch the Russells' cattle branding. But Josie could never talk her father into letting Stella come over. He said it was too dangerous.

Stella sat up straighter, starting to feel a little excited and nervous.

"Things may get a bit wild." Anya's eyes were on the road, looking for her turnoff. "You're going to have two jobs."

"Tell me now."

"One, fill syringes. I'll show you how much vaccine each one gets."

"No problem."

"Two—and this is the most important thing— you need to stay out of the cattle's way. I definitely don't want you to get trampled by some frantic cow."

"Okay." Stella felt a tiny twinge of uneasiness. But she knew Anya wouldn't let her get hurt.

The Homesick Ranch was a smallish cattle ranch about forty miles north of town. Stella had ridden by it dozens of times on her way into Bozeman with her parents. Usually, all she saw of the ranch was an acre of split log fence and open fields that zipped by at sixty-five miles an hour.

Anya turned into the drive. Stella could see a big, low ranch house set in the middle of a valley. The barn and stable were another mile farther in from the road.

Stella saw three men and twice as many dogs hanging around outside the barn. They all looked over as Anya drove up. They had been waiting for her.

Anya put the car into PARK and climbed out. "Howdy, Rib! Loren. Dutch."

Stella hurried to get out.

The grown-ups all shook hands. They talked about the dry weather for a few minutes. Three weeks and no rain. Then Anya introduced Stella to the men. Rib was older—about the same age as Stella's grandfather. He had blue eyes and a salt-and-pepper beard. Loren looked like him, only younger. Dutch was just a teenager. He was a hired hand.

"Dutch, get the horse," Rib said. He was clearly in charge. "I'll help these ladies with their gear."

"Great." Anya moved around to the back of her truck and began pulling out boxes holding syringes, bottles of vaccine, and other gear. They carried everything down to an old wooden table that stood next to a blazing fire. A couple of branding irons were standing nearby in a pail of sand.

About a hundred head of cattle were crowded into the corral outside the barn. They were like a great brown-and-white sea, constantly in motion.

"Start out just watching," Anya said.

Stella nodded.

Dutch rode into the corral on a big roan gelding. Anya told Stella the horse was a "cutter"—trained to separate cows from the herd.

The cattle tried to move away from the horse. They raised their heads and snorted in panic. The air filled with the dust they kicked up as they rushed from one side of the corral to the other. In the confusion, cows became separated from their calves.

"Why are they so freaked out?" Stella shouted. The terrified cattle were making an awful racket. Calves bleated. Cows bellowed.

"They're wild animals!" Anya yelled back. "Some of these calves never saw a person before they were rounded up yesterday."

"The herd only sees us a few times a year!" Rib shouted.

Stella felt like sticking her fingers in her ears. She didn't know if she should feel sorry for the cattle because they seemed so frightened or feel impatient with them because they were making

Her calf was standing a few feet away—as if he realized something strange was going on.

Then—almost in slow motion—the cow crashed over on to her side.

Stella stared at the capsized cow for a moment. Then she turned and ran back to where Anya was working.

"Anya. A cow just collapsed!"

"Collapsed?"

"Passed out!"

"Hold it up, Rib," Anya shouted. "It sounds like one of the calves may have had an allergic reaction to the vaccine. Where's the calf, Stella?"

"Over here. But it's not a calf. It's a cow."

Now Stella was running. Everyone was following her. Anya saw the cow and dropped to her knees next to her. She leaned forward and put an ear against the cow's stomach.

"Nothing," Anya announced.

"Milk fever?" Rib asked.

"Milk fever," Anya confirmed. "Don't see it much in beef cows."

She sat up and looked at Stella. "Run to the truck and get me a bottle of calcium gluconate. It's a white bottle. Rib, better get a sling out here. We'll want to support her when she gets up."

"Sure thing." Rib trotted off toward the corral.

Stella headed for the truck. She found the calcium gluconate without too much trouble and ran back. Loren, Dutch, and Rib were all working on the cow. They had laid a big strap on the ground. Stella watched as they grabbed the cow's hooves and pulled her onto the strap.

Anya took the calcium gluconate and syringe from Stella without even looking at her. She injected the cow.

Stella stood a few feet away, feeling certain that the cow was going to die. What would happen to her calf then? She didn't understand why Rib and Anya seemed so calm. Some strange disease had knocked this cow down.

The cow suddenly raised her head.

Stella blinked, not believing it.

Then it happened again! The cow lifted her head. She gazed at Stella as if wondering "What am I doing down here?"

"I think she's getting up!" Stella said.

The cow laid her head down and shifted onto her belly.

"Get ready, boys!" Rib called. "She's coming up."

Loren and Dutch were on either side of the cow. They were each holding one side of the strap. The cow got her front feet under her. Loren and Dutch hauled on the strap.

The material tightened up under the cow's stomach. Just like that, she was up on all fours.

Anya came forward and looked into her eyes. The cow gazed calmly back. "She seems steady. Try letting go of the strap."

Cautiously at first, Loren and Dutch loosened the strap.

The cow stayed on her feet.

Anya nodded.

Loren and Dutch let the strap drop. Dutch pulled it out of the way.

The cow's calf took a step toward her.

Rib clapped his hands. "Well, since we're taking a break anyway, who needs a drink?"

"A soda would be great," Anya said. "And I want to keep an eye on this cow for ten minutes. She may need another injection."

The men moved off toward the house.

"I don't believe it," Stella told Anya.

Anya smiled. "Pretty dramatic, huh?"

"What was wrong with her?"

"Milk fever. Sometimes cows that are nursing lose too much calcium, and they basically faint. Injecting them with a dose of calcium usually brings them back."

"The cow has a fever?"

"No. That's just what people call this condition. The proper term is hypocalcemia."

"What's up with the sling?"

"That helps keep the cow from tearing a muscle or fracturing a bone when she stands up. Sometimes they struggle. This gal had an easy time of it."

It was true. The cow was already tearing at the grass. She seemed completely recovered. Stella felt happy. Really happy. Being a veterinarian was just so great. Anya had made the cow better without even breaking a sweat. If she hadn't been here, the cow would have been dead—er, meat.

Stella gave Anya a sudden hug.

Anya laughed. "What's that for?"

Anya's cell phone bleeped. She unsnapped it from her belt and pressed a button. "Hello? Oh, hey. What's happening?"

"It's your mom," Anya whispered to Stella.

"What's happening?" Stella demanded. "Did they find Juliet and the pups?"

"Shhh," Anya said.

Stella covered her mouth with both hands. "Oops."

She'd forgotten that her mother's mission was supposed to be a secret—not that anyone but Anya could have heard her.

Norma seemed to be telling Anya a long story.

Anya was nodding and saying "hmm hmm" a lot.

Stella had no idea what they were talking about. She couldn't even tell if the news was good or bad. She hopped from foot to foot and tried to be patient.

Anya finally switched off the phone. But by then, Rib was coming back across the field. He was carrying a couple of cans of soda.

"What did she say?" Stella whispered. "Tell me quick!"

Anya sighed. "Things aren't going that well. She and Mack set a leg hold trap near where you and Norma saw the pups. The trap worked like a charm. It caught Juliet without giving her a scratch."

"So what's the problem?" Stella asked. "Did she get away or something?"

"Nope. Norma and Mack drugged her and loaded her into the helicopter without a hitch."

Rib was only a hundred feet away.

"So what's the problem?" Stella whispered urgently.

"No pups," Anya said quickly.

Rib was smiling as he approached. "Hello! How's our patient doing?"

Stella had actually forgotten about the cow. She spun around and took a look. The cow was just fine. She and her calf had moved a dozen feet away. They were totally back to normal.

Rib held out a Coke, and Stella took it. She popped it open.

Anya took a sip out of her own can. "Let's get back to work," she suggested.

"I'm game," Rib said.

They started back to the corral. Stella had about a thousand questions for Anya. Most urgently: What did she mean—no pups? Stella had seen the pups herself. Had they somehow gotten lost?

Rib called to Loren and Dutch, who were sitting on the top rail of the corral fence. They jumped up and got back into position.

"Oh, Stella," Anya said. "You forgot to get those new syringes."

"Sorry," Stella said. "I'll get them now."

She started toward the truck. Then she had an idea. "Anya—may I borrow your phone?" she asked.

"Sure." Anya handed it to her with a wink.

Stella hurried to the truck. She climbed inside where she could get some privacy and dialed her mom's number. It rang.

"Hello?"

"Mom, it's Stella. What's going on?"

"The pups are gone. We think Juliet hid them."

• 9 •

Stella stared out of Anya's dusty windshield at Rib's red barn. She pressed the cell phone against her ear. Had she misunderstood?

"Why would Juliet hide her pups?" Stella asked.

"I don't know." Norma's voice was kind of flat, as if she were very tired, or dejected.

"Don't sound so sad, Mom. You'll find them."

"Well, we're going to try. We've plotted all of the places Juliet's signal has been picked up over the past twenty-four hours. We found a hot spot on the other side of Mount Edna. Looks like she moved the pups over there."

"Have you checked it out yet?"

"No."

"Why not? Aren't the pups in danger without their mom?"

"Yes, they are. But there's a problem."

"What problem?"

"Juliet's new hangout isn't on public land."

"Is it on the Russells' land?" Stella guessed.

"Yup."

"So ask Mr. Russell if you can look there!" Stella said.

"I left him a message an hour ago." Norma's tone was level. "He hasn't returned my call yet."

"Then I'll talk to Josie!"

"I don't think that's a good idea. Let's give Mr. Russell some time to get back to me."

"And until then—what do we do?"

"Wait."

Stella thought about that part of the Russells' land. Pasture land was cleared a few hundred yards up the mountainside. The fence ran right against the tree line.

The Russells owned land clear up to the summit, but the terrain was too steep for cattle. So they'd left the forest on the upper half intact. Josie said they'd lost several calves near the fence. Mountain lions could hide in the thick undergrowth and attack livestock far from the ranch buildings.

"A mountain lion could be gobbling down the

pups right now," Stella insisted. "We have to do something. We can't just let them die."

"Well, we can't turn a man's daughter against him either," Norma said. "Now I don't want you causing trouble in that family."

Stella stared down at the box of syringes in her lap. Anya probably needed them. She should get back.

"I'd better go," Stella told her mother sullenly.

"Okay, Muffin. And don't sound so glum. We're doing everything we can."

Norma sounded like she was trying to cheer Stella up. But Stella could tell that she was worried.

"I know. Don't worry about me."

Stella told herself to trust her mom. Norma usually knew how to handle things. After all, she helped get the wolves reintroduced in the first place.

Still, Stella felt awful as she climbed out of the truck and delivered the syringes to Anya. They spent the rest of the afternoon vaccinating and branding calves. Anya dropped Stella off at home just in time for her to take Rufus to obedience school.

The obedience school was held in a small park right in the center of town. Zack, the instructor, liked dogs a whole lot, and he seemed to really understand them. He'd learned dog training from actual monks who lived in New York State. Monks, as in taking vows of silence, living in cells, and praying all the time.

Besides doing all that stuff, these monks also raised German shepherds and wrote best-selling books about dog training and understanding your dog's *spirit*. Stella thought it sounded a bit wacky, but Zack's class drew in dog owners from all over Montana. Anya had recommended Zack highly.

Stella loved the classes. Seeing all the different dogs together made her happy. Their owners were funny, too.

Mr. Shaw from the library had an English pointer named Blue.

Harold, who owned the Texaco station in town, came with Sky, a Scottish terrier.

A teenaged girl named Becky owned a bullmastiff she called Hank.

Rufus was the smallest dog.

Stella was the youngest owner.

"Hello, Stella!" Zack greeted her. He was a small, thin man with close-cropped gray hair. Stella thought he looked like a monk. No robe, though. He wore a T-shirt, shorts, and sandals. "How is Rufus doing with the sit?"

"Not that well," Stella admitted. "He keeps

looking at me like he doesn't understand *why* he should sit."

"And why should he?"

"Because I want him to!"

"And why do you want him to?"

"Because I—I guess I don't know why."

Zack smiled benevolently. "Class!" he called quietly. "Everyone, listen up. I think Stella discovered something important while working with Rufus this week."

"I did?" Stella looked at Becky and shrugged. She had no idea what Zack was talking about.

"Yes." Zack was still smiling. "You discovered that teaching Rufus to simply obey an order isn't easy. And do you know why it isn't easy?"

Stella shook her head. She was still in the dark.

"Because you didn't really want to succeed!"

"I didn't?"

"No. And it's because you truly love Rufus."

Stella looked down at Rufus's sweet furry face. His pink tongue was hanging out of one side of his mouth. His tail started going as soon as she looked at him. She did love Rufus. But she still didn't have any idea what Zack was talking about.

"How can I explain this?" Zack was quiet for a moment, organizing his thoughts.

Stella gave Rufus a little more leash. He went over and gave Sky a sniff.

"Those of you who are parents," Zack said. "I want you to think of training your dog in the same way you think about raising your children. Now you don't want to teach your kids to blindly obey orders. The same goes for your dog. You want a dog that can think."

Harold and Mr. Shaw were nodding knowingly.

"Once in a while, without meaning to, we might give our dogs a command that could harm them." Zack looked at Stella. "Imagine calling Rufus from across the street—just as a truck was lumbering down the road. You wouldn't want Rufus to follow an order like that."

"No way," Stella said.

"That's why you should never punish your dog," Zack said. "We don't want them to be good little soldiers. We want them to keep thinking—thinking about how they can please us. Now let's show Rufus how happy it makes you when he sits."

Stella was only half-paying attention. She was thinking about her own parents. Were Norma and Jack teaching her to think for herself?

Not this afternoon, Stella decided. Norma had pretty much told her to stand up and fly straight. Follow orders. And the thing that bothered Stella was that she was almost certain her mother was wrong.

Waiting for Mr. Russell to call back was the wrong thing to do.

How could they just wait when so much was at stake? They were risking the lives of eight little wolf pups—the first wolf pups born in Goldenrock in seventy years.

And yet . . .

The wolves had come between Stella and Josie in the past. Josie was a ranch kid. She would just never admit that the wolves deserved another chance.

Maybe talking to Josie wasn't the answer.

Josie wouldn't help the wolves if it meant going against her father. And Norma had told Stella not to talk to Josie.

But Norma hadn't said anything about talking to Mr. Russell.

And that was exactly what Stella decided to do.

• 10 •

Obedience school ended fifty minutes later. Rufus still wasn't sitting on command. But Stella figured that was because she was having such a hard time concentrating.

Usually, Stella let Rufus hang out at the park for a while and play with the other dogs. After all that time in class, she figured he deserved a little recess. And he loved to play at fighting with the other dogs. Especially Sky, the Scottie. Sky wasn't all that much bigger than Rufus.

But Stella didn't have any time to waste that afternoon. She scooped Rufus up immediately and put him in the basket on her bicycle.

Rufus tried to jump out. But he stopped as soon as Stella was in motion.

The Russells' ranch was a twenty-minute bike ride outside town. The closer Stella got, the more nervous she felt. She tried to figure out what she would say to Mr. Russell. How would she convince him to let her mother onto his property?

Nothing she came up with sounded like it would work.

Mr. Russell wasn't mean exactly, but he wasn't the type of father who stood around and asked you about your day. He always seemed busy and preoccupied. Too busy and preoccupied to spend time arguing with a kid.

Still, Stella felt like she had to try. It was like Jared and the goldfish. She realized that she might not be able to save the wolf pups, but she wanted to know that she had done everything possible.

Stella took a deep breath as she turned her bike up the Russells' driveway. She was concentrating on what she was going to say, which was why she didn't notice Anya's truck at first.

When she *did* notice it, something about the way the truck was parked made Stella's heart skip a beat. The angle was strange—as if Anya had jerked to a stop quickly.

Stella got off her bike. She tied Rufus's leash to a tree. Then she rushed into the barn.

Voices.

Frantic talk was coming from one of the horse stalls. Stella recognized Anya's, Mr. Russell's, and Josie's voices. She started to run.

Josie was standing outside Esmeralda's box. So was Clem.

Oh no, Stella thought. *What's wrong with Esme?* Esme was the Russells' favorite mare. She was a beautiful chestnut quarter house with a kind face and uncanny intelligence.

Stella stopped next to Josie and quickly took in the scene. Anya and Mr. Russell were inside the box. They were half-blocking Stella's view. But it didn't take her long to decide Esme was fine. Well, sort of fine. She focused one big black eye on Stella, and Stella could have sworn she looked scared.

Esme wasn't hurt. But Gus, her colt, was. Gus was about seven weeks old. He was a jet-black colt. He was playful. And usually rather calm.

But not now. Now his eyes were wild with fear. He was bucking and kicking. Mr. Russell had his arms wrapped around him. But Gus was tossing his head and kicking with his forelegs.

"Dad—want me to get a twitch?" Clem asked.

A twitch was a loop of chain on a handle, and was used to restrain a horse. The chain went over the horse's nose. You twisted it until it was snug. Twitches looked like they hurt. Horse people used them all the time, but Stella hated them. They made *her* twitch.

"No!" Josie yelled. "Clem, don't you hurt him!"

"I'm trying to keep *him* from hurting Dad!"

"I'm all right," Mr. Russell grunted.

Stella grabbed Josie's arm. "What's going on?"

"We don't know!"

"I've got to examine his legs!" Anya told Mr. Russell. "Got him? Okay?"

"Yes, yes! Just do it!"

Stella held her breath as Anya ran her fingers over the colt's legs. She'd seen something like this before—a horse with hives. But that horse had been covered with bumps. And Gus's flesh was smooth. What *was* this?

Anya shook her head, looking baffled. "Nothing! Wait—let me try his nose." She grasped the terrified colt's head firmly in her right hand and explored his flesh with her left fingertips.

"Here it is! Yes—a snakebite. Looks like . . . a rattler."

Rattlesnakes were poisonous. Their fangs shot venom.

"So what's the big deal?" Clem demanded. "Snake bites usually don't bother horses much."

Anya was already coming out of the box. "True. But in a colt Gus's size, they can be deadly."

"Where are you going?" Josie sounded a bit panicked.

"I've got some anti-venom in my truck," Anya said.

"I'll get it," Stella offered.

"That's okay," Anya said. "I can find it faster. You all stay here and keep that colt calm. Gus will absorb the toxin more quickly if he's excited or struggling."

• 11 •

Suddenly Josie was in charge. "Let him go, Dad. And come out of there. Gus doesn't know you that well."

Mr. Russell looked as if he didn't like being ordered around. But he did what Josie told him to do.

Josie went into the box alone. She knelt down next to Gus and began whispering in his ear. The colt responded to her familiar voice. He stopped kicking. But his eyes were still wide with fear.

Anya was back a moment later. She gently ran her hand along the colt's neck. Then she pushed a thumb into it. A vein appeared. Anya tapped her fingers against Gus's neck so that he wouldn't be surprised by the needle prick. She slowly injected the anti-venom.

"Is he going to be okay?" Josie asked.

"Sure thing." Anya gave Josie a wink.

Stella felt her panic subside a bit. The crisis seemed to be over. She watched as Anya cleaned out Gus's bite. The colt blinked sleepily. He was suddenly much more calm. Esme nuzzled him with her muzzle. Things in the barn felt peaceful—for about two seconds. Then Josie looked over and gave Stella a puzzled look.

"What are you doing here?"

Stella was unprepared for the question. "I—I, well . . ." She took a deep breath and looked at Mr. Russell. "I wanted to talk to you."

"What about?" Mr. Russell sounded almost angry.

Stella swallowed hard. She'd known asking Mr. Russell would be difficult. And that was *before* she'd realized she was going to have to ask him in front of Josie, Clem, and Anya.

Well, maybe the best thing was just to come out with it. "I want you to give my mom permission to search for a litter of wolf pups on your land."

"Wolf . . . pups?" Clem's mouth was practically hanging open. Mr. Russell looked almost as sur-

prised. Josie seemed a bit nervous—as if she was expecting trouble.

Stella couldn't see Anya's face because Anya was still turned toward Gus. But something about her posture made Stella think she disapproved. Had Norma told Anya that Stella was supposed to butt out? Or was she just angry because Stella had told the Russells about the pups?

"I'm sure you heard about the wolf that was shot," Stella hurried on. "Well, these are his pups. Mom decided to bring the mother wolf and the pups back to their pen in Goldenrock. She got the mother okay, but the pups are on your land."

"Here?" Josie looked around as if she expected a litter of wolf pups to materialize right in the barn.

"Up on Mount Edna," Stella explained.

"Where?" Clem demanded.

Stella hesitated. She couldn't quite convince herself to trust Clem. Some tiny part of her still suspected that he was involved in Romeo's shooting.

"I'm . . . not sure," Stella said. "But my mom knows. And I'm sure she could get the pups . . ."

She let her voice trail off because Mr. Russell was shaking his head slowly.

"I'm not doing a thing to help those wolves,"

Mr. Russell said. He sounded as if he'd never change his mind, not in a million years. "I'd sooner shoot myself in the foot."

At that particular moment, Stella wouldn't have minded helping him. She bit her lip and forced herself not to freak out. She hadn't thought this was going to be easy. She tried to remember some of the arguments she'd thought of on the bike ride over.

Stella forced herself to shrug. "I'm surprised you want a pack of wolf pups camping out on your land," she said. "You know, they're probably going to grow fast."

Yeah, right, Stella thought. *If they don't die first. If they hadn't died already.*

"We won't let 'em camp out here," Clem said. "We'll just shoot 'em."

"That's against the law!" Stella said hotly. Now she was worried—worried that she had told Clem too much. Worried that he would make sure the pups died just like their father had.

"It's only illegal if you get caught," Clem said. "Shoot up, shovel up, and shut up. That's my motto."

Ordinarily it would have been hard to ignore him, but Stella was focusing on Mr. Russell.

Mr. Russell was frowning uncertainly.

Stella could tell how much he hated the idea of a bunch of wolves on his property.

"I don't want government employees on my land," Mr. Russell said slowly, thinking it over. "But it's okay if Anya rides up and gets the pups."

"No!" Josie howled. "Gus needs Anya here."

Stella opened her mouth to argue. But she closed it without saying a word. Gus was awfully important to Josie. If Anya needed to stay, then she should stay.

"Daddy," Josie said. "How about I go up Mount Edna and get the pups? Then Anya can stay down here."

"Sure," Stella said. "We can go together!" She shot Josie a grateful smile.

But Mr. Russell was shaking his head again. "I don't want you girls going up on that mountain alone. Clem, go with 'em."

Anya's eyes widened.

Stella felt like protesting, but she knew better than to press her luck. "Thanks," she said through gritted teeth.

Stella was determined to save the wolf pups.

Whatever it took.

• 12 •

Stella locked herself in Anya's truck and called her mom. Norma wasn't thrilled with the idea of Stella, Josie, and Clem going after the pups, but Stella finally convinced her mom that Mr. Russell's way was the only way. Norma reluctantly gave Stella directions for finding the pups.

Half an hour later, they were on their way.

Stella was riding Honey, a horse who was almost as old as she was. She didn't ride much, but she felt comfortable on the gentle mare.

Josie's horse was almost as old. Her name was Sally, and she belonged to Josie's mom before she died.

Clem was on a three-year-old gelding named

Powderkeg. His name was more wishful thinking than anything. He didn't have much spark.

Even though they were only planning to be gone a few hours, they had come prepared. Their saddlebags were full of supplies—food, watch, compass, map, gloves, cell phone, first-aid kit. And they had an old cloth sleeping bag. That was what Norma suggested they carry the pups in.

Stella was feeling pretty good as they started across the huge pasture toward the mountain. So what if they had a two-hour ride ahead of them? She liked riding. The truth was, she was feeling a bit smug. She'd thought for herself, just like Zack had suggested, and now the pups had a chance.

Then she noticed the rifle. The big weapon was in a holster right near Clem's right leg. Stella felt a twinge of doubt. A very big twinge. Were they really going to save the pups? Or was Clem planning on shooting them?

Stella gently pulled back on Honey's reins and the mare dropped into a slow walk.

Clem pulled ahead almost instantly.

"Josie!" Stella called quietly.

Josie heard her. She slowed Sally and waited until Stella and Honey caught up.

"What's Clem doing with that rifle?" Stella demanded.

Josie's expression was blank. She shrugged. "He always rides with it. For safety."

"Safety against what? Rabid rabbits?"

Josie rolled her eyes. "Just relax. Clem's not going to shoot your precious pups."

"He'd better not."

"Relax." Josie gave Sally a little kick and rode ahead.

What could Stella do? She followed the others, trying not to worry. She told herself that if Clem harmed any of the wolves, she'd have Assistant Sheriff Rose throw him into some awful juvenile hall.

Half an hour later, they rode up to the fence that divided the gently sloping pasture from the woods. There wasn't a gate or opening in the fence, so they had to leave the horses in the pasture.

They dismounted, tied the horses to the fence, and gave them some water. They gathered their gear. Stella noticed that Clem brought the rifle.

"So how are we supposed to find a bunch of wild animals out in the woods?" Clem asked.

"I have directions," Stella said. She pulled out her map and compass. Jack and Norma had taught her how to navigate in the woods practically as soon as she'd learned to walk. She put the compass on the map and got her bearings. "We need to walk Northeast."

Clem stared at her. "Which way is that?"

Josie smirked. "I told you not to drop out of Boy Scouts."

Stella studied her compass and then looked ahead. "See that lighting-struck aspen tree? We need to get there. Then I'll take my bearings again."

Clem started trudging toward the tree. "Great. I feel lost already. Maybe we should have brought that bloodhound of yours." Rufus was still down in the valley. Anya had promised to keep an eye on him.

"Clem," Josie said in a warning tone. "Don't pick on Rufus."

Stella shot Josie a look. "Right. Like *you* never pick on Rufus."

"That's different," Josie said. "I'm practically Rufus's aunt. I'm allowed to tease him."

Stella forced a smile. She was tense. Tense about getting lost. Tense about finding the wolf pups. And tense about what would happen when they *did* find them. If Clem tried to hurt the pups, how could Stella stop him?

They reached the aspen tree. Stella lined her compass up again. She picked another land-mark—a rock covered with moss. When they reached the rock, Stella picked another landmark.

They weren't getting anywhere fast. Stella felt impatient, but she knew it was important to be careful and to keep on the right course.

She was extremely relieved twenty minutes later when they finally reached the right place. At least, Stella *thought* it was the right place.

"This is it," Stella announced. She turned in a slow circle. They were standing on top of a rocky outcropping. You could see the valley through a break in the trees. The summit was still another quarter mile above them.

"Great," Clem said. He sat down in a sunny spot and leaned back against the rock. He tipped his hat forward.

Josie kicked his boot. "What are you doing?"

"Napping. Dad said I had to come with you. He didn't say anything about *helping* you."

"Creep."

"That's me," Clem said with satisfaction. He closed his eyes.

Stella didn't mind. In fact, she didn't really want Clem's help. She wanted Clem, and his rifle, to stay as far away from the pups as possible.

A few feet away was a tree with a rotted-out trunk. Maybe the pups were down there. Stella went over, got down on her hands and knees, and peered inside. She didn't see anything but a couple of termites.

What if the pups were hiding?

What if they were scared of them?

They'd never find the pups if they hunkered back in some little hole and hid.

Then Stella remembered her mother's trick. The sound she had made. Stella tried it. A breathy kind of grunt.

"What was that?" Josie asked.

"The sound a mother wolf makes when she comes back to the den."

"Really?" Josie laughed.

"Well, I'm trying! Now hush up."

Stella kept making the mother-wolf noise. After a while, Josie joined in. Stella had no idea if they sounded anything like a real wolf. Probably not.

She got down and looked in small openings between the rocks. Then she heard something. A sound like little creatures playing, climbing over each other. A breathy kind of grunt.

The next second they tumbled out. A whole gang of wolf pups piled out of a crevice between a couple of big boulders.

"Josie—look," Stella whispered.

The pups stood in the pine-needle–covered clearing, surrounded by scrubby trees. A couple of gray ones. One that was completely black. One with white fur on his front paws.

Stella froze.

Intelligent yellow eyes were staring up at her. The pups' eyes had opened! They were silent. Then one pup let out a shrill puppy bark.

The pups dashed in all directions. Before Stella could react, they were gone. Hidden here and there in the tumble of rocks and boulders.

"Get them!" Stella told Josie.

Stella could see a bit of tail sticking out of a pile of rocks close to her. She reached in and pulled out a gray pup. He instantly tried to bite her.

Josie started to yank gear out of her bag. "Here's the sleeping bag," she said, shaking it out. "And put on these gloves."

Stella lowered the pup into the bag. She pulled on gloves. So did Josie.

One by one they pulled pups out of tiny hiding places, and plopped them into the sleeping bag. Stella kept count. Half an hour later, they were up to seven.

"Is that all of them?" Josie asked.

"I'm not sure," Stella said. "When Mom and I first saw the pups we couldn't tell if there were seven or eight."

"So I bet we got them all," Josie said. She sounded ready to leave.

Stella hesitated. Josie was probably right. But . . .

What if there were eight pups? Stella couldn't stand the thought of leaving one behind.

"Let me check one more time," Stella said. They'd found four of the pups quivering together in a skinny rock crevice. Stella got down on her belly and reached in one more time.

"Anything?" Josie asked.

"No—" Stella gasped. "Yes! I just felt a tiny piece of fur."

"Are you sure?"

"Positive." Stella grunted as she tried to shove her arm farther in. Her arm was too big to reach all the way to the back. But she felt a snatch of fur—fur that was scooting away from her. "My arm is too—big!"

"Then you'd better give up." Clem had appeared. He stood looking down at Stella. "It'll be dark in a couple of hours. Time to go."

"Not until we get the last pup," Stella said. She shoved her arm with all of her might. Too tight. The rock wouldn't let her in.

"I'll give you two minutes," Clem said.

Stella relaxed and tried to think. Somehow she

felt as if she'd been in a similar spot not too long ago.

It came to her in a flash.

Bruiser, the piglet.

"Maybe we can lure the pup out with a scrap of meat," Stella suggested.

"Ham sandwich?" Josie asked.

Stella nodded.

Josie pulled the sandwich out of her bag and gave Stella a piece of ham. Stella crammed the meat into the crevice. She waited.

"Has it occurred to you that this pup hasn't been weaned yet?" Clem asked.

"We're doing our best here!" Stella shouted.

Clem shrugged. "Your two minutes are up. I'm heading back to the horses."

"You don't know the way," Stella said.

"Yes, I do. Down. Once I get to the pasture, finding the horses will be easy."

Stella felt completely defeated. "We can't just leave the pup," she said hopelessly. "He'll starve all alone."

Josie looked off in the direction Clem was heading.

"Are you coming or what?" Clem shouted back.

Josie looked at Stella. She seemed to make up her mind. She came forward, taking off her gloves. "Get out of the way."

Stella scooted back.

Josie was about a head shorter than Stella. Her arms were much skinnier. She laid down on her belly and put her arm into the crevice. "It's awfully tight . . ."

"Can you reach him?"

"I . . . think . . . I've got his tail!"

Josie pulled her arm out. She had a tiny gray pup by the tail. He was in full resistance mode. His needlelike claws were out, trying to hold onto the smooth rock.

"Your knuckles are all bloody," Stella said.

"I told you it was tight."

Stella took the pup and gave him a quick hug. She knew she never would have reached him without Josie's help.

"Thanks," Stella said. "For everything—I mean, you didn't have to help me help the wolves."

Josie shrugged. "I owed you one. At least one!"

They hiked down to the horses. Clem was waiting for them, his expression stormy. They rode out. When they got back to the ranch two hours later, Anya was there to check on Gus. She said the colt was completely out of danger.

Mr. Russell was out in the pastures, taking care of some chores. Stella quickly helped Josie unsaddle the horses and get them settled in the barn. Then she gave her friend a hug good-bye.

Anya put the pups in her truck. They were still in their sleeping bag. She drove Stella into town, where Norma was waiting at the clinic. Before midnight that night, Juliet was reunited with her pups. They were all settled in at the pen, safe back in the park.

Stella felt terrific. Especially when her mom told her that Morehouse, that Fish and Wildlife guy, had arrested someone for shooting Romeo. The shooter's name was Lincoln Tyler. He was a local man who worked at one of the sawmills.

It hadn't been Clem after all.

But Stella couldn't stop thinking about Clem's rifle and wondering why he had brought it up Mount Edna.

Maybe Clem hadn't shot Romeo.

But that didn't mean he hadn't wanted to.

Besides, a lot of people in Gateway thought Lincoln Tyler was a hero.

Stella also couldn't help worrying about the rest of the wolves—the ones that were still running free out in the park. She hoped they were safe.

CATTLE BRANDING

How did you feel when you read about branding in this story? Did it make you cringe?

Branding seems cruel to many people. It's easy to imagine how much it would hurt to have hot metal held against your skin. And it's only natural to be uncomfortable with the idea of cattle suffering.

Why is branding necessary?

Ranchers are concerned with the well-being of cattle, too. After all, ranchers rely on cattle for their living. And most ranchers like cows—otherwise, why would they spend their lives surrounded by them?

When it comes to cows, ranchers are experts—and they claim that cattle aren't overly bothered by branding. A properly applied brand does hurt the calf, but not as much as you might think. Cowhide is much thicker than human skin. Most calves recover quickly. Sometimes they start grazing only minutes after being branded.

Ranchers also say that branding their animals is necessary. Here are three reasons why:

1) Cows of the same breed look alike.
2) Cows like to break out of fences.
3) Unmarked cows are easy pickings for rustlers—people who steal livestock.

A brand is a tool that allows a rancher to identify his or her stock—even if it's currently strolling down the road looking for a nice patch of grass. This is especially important when you consider that about thirty-three *million* cows live in the United States.

Tradition

But branding is more than just practical. It's also a ranching tradition—a cherished part of western culture. Many ranching families are extraordinarily proud of their brands—symbols they've chosen as their own. They carve their brands onto belts and boots, monogram them onto their clothes, and print them on their stationery. Different members of ranching families sometimes have their own unique brands. What would your brand look like?

How to read a brand

Learning to read brands is a bit like learning to read a foreign language. Here are some secrets to help you break the code.

Brands are read from left to right, top to bottom, and outside inward. In addition to letters and numbers, some common symbols include:

▬ The bar
◯ The circle

A simple brand might look something like this Ō and be read "bar zero," or "bar none." Many, many simple brands can be made by mixing up letters, symbols, and numbers. The Homesick Ranch's brand described in this story is a simple or "standing" ℞. Ranch folks like Josie would read this as R S "connected" since the letters are smashed right up against each other.

Over the years, ranchers have devised ways to make their brands fancier and more complicated.

The Homesick Ranch brand could be "lazy," laid down on its side and look like this: ╫

A "crazy" Homesick Ranch brand might be upside down ⊊Я or backward Ɔᴚ or both ℔Ɽ.

Getting dizzy yet?
Well, there's more!

ᒲ This E brand is "walking." If I had some cows, this might be a good brand for me since my name starts with an "e" and I walk everywhere I go.

V See those little "wings" on this V? That's what makes this a "flying" V. Some poetic ranch hands might read it "winged victory."

ᴍ This M is "running." Brands without sharp edges are easier to make with primitive branding irons called running irons—which are basically just steel bars that are used like a hot pencil. More elaborate brands are made with stamping irons, which are crafted by ironsmiths.

Here is the brand used by one of the most famous stockmen in America. B̄Q̄ Can you guess how to read it? That's right. It's bar BQ—or barbecue!

Join in All the Daring
Environmental Adventures with

Parsons Point lighthouse on the Atlantic coast, home to cousins Dana and Tyler Chapin, is part of Project Neptune, a nonprofit operation that works with sick and injured sea animals.

DANGER ON CRAB ISLAND
79488-8/$3.99 US/$4.99 Can

DISASTER AT PARSONS POINT
79489-6/$3.99 US/$4.99 Can

THE DOLPHIN TRAP
79490-X/$3.99 US/$4.99 Can

STRANDING ON CEDAR POINT
79492-6/$3.99 US/$4.99 Can

HURRICANE RESCUE
80252-X/$3.99 US/$4.99 Can

RED TIDE ALERT
80253-8/$3.99 US/$4.99 Can

Read all of Avi's
Tales from Dimwood Forest

POPPY
72769-2/$4.99 US/$6.99 Can

POPPY AND RYE
79717-8/$4.99 US/$6.99 Can

RAGWEED
97690-0/$15.00 US/$22.00 Can

ERETH'S BIRTHDAY

Coming in hardcover in May 2000

Read All the Stories by
Beverly Cleary